'He gave orders
that they were
not to get any hot
glum pudding in
flames, for fear
the spirits in their
innards might
catch fire . . .'

D1649349

NIKOLAY SEMYONOVICH LESKOV
Born 1831, Oryol, Russia
Died 1895, Saint Petersburg, Russia

'The Steel Flea' was first published in Russian in 1881.

LESKOV IN PENGUIN CLASSICS
*Russian Short Stories from Pushkin to Buida*
*Lady Macbeth of Mtsensk and Other Stories*

# NIKOLAY LESKOV

## The Steel Flea

Translated by
William Edgerton

PENGUIN BOOKS

PENGUIN CLASSICS

UK | USA | Canada | Ireland | Australia
India | New Zealand | South Africa

Penguin Books is part of the Penguin Random House group of companies
whose addresses can be found at global.penguinrandomhouse.com.

This edition published in Penguin Classics 2015
014

Translation copyright © The Estate of William Edgerton, 1969, 2015

The moral right of the translator has been asserted

Set in 9.5/13 pt Baskerville 10 Pro
Typeset by Jouve (UK), Milton Keynes

Printed and bound in Great Britain by Clays Ltd, Elcograf S.p.A.

A CIP catalogue record for this book is available from the British Library

ISBN: 978–0–141–39739–9

www.greenpenguin.co.uk

MIX
Paper from
responsible sources
FSC® C018179

Penguin Random House is committed to a
sustainable future for our business, our readers
and our planet. This book is made from Forest
Stewardship Council® certified paper.

# The Steel Flea

## (The Tale of the Cross-Eyed, Left-Handed Gunsmith from Tula and the Steel Flea)

### 1

When Emperor Aleksandr the First had finished the Council of Vienna he decided he would like to take a trip around Europe and look at the marvels in the different countries. He travelled through all the nations, and everywhere his friendliness always helped him get into the most intimidating conversations with all kinds of people, and everybody would amaze him with one thing or another and try to win him over to their side. But along with him was the Don Cossack Platov, who didn't like all this persuasion; he hankered to get back to his farm, and he kept trying to talk the Emperor into going home. And if Platov noticed the Emperor getting really interested in something foreign, then just as soon as all the guides stopped talking for a minute, Platov would pop up and say this, that and the other, telling them ours at home was just as good, and one way or another he would get their minds onto something else.

The Englishmen knew this, and they thought up all kinds of shifty tricks for the Emperor's visit, so as to get him in their power with their outlandishness and get his mind off the Russians, and in a lot of cases they managed it, especially at their big meetings, where Platov couldn't say everything completely in French. But then he was not very much interested in that, since he was a married man and looked on all French conversations as trifles not worthy of serious imagination. And when the Englishmen started inviting the Emperor into all their store houses, gun works and soapy-rope factories, so as to show how much better they were than us in everything and then brag about it, Platov said to himself, 'Well, this has gone far enough. I've put up with it so far, but I can't take any more. Maybe I'll succeed and maybe I'll fail, but at least I won't go back on my own people.'

And he had no sooner said this to himself than the Emperor told him, 'Tomorrow you and I are going to look at their military museum. There they've got such natures of perfection that just as soon as you've seen them you'll agree that we Russians with our significance don't mean a thing.'

Platov said nothing in reply to the Emperor, but just stuck his humpbacked nose down into his shaggy felt overcoat and went to his room. He told his orderly to get a bottle of Caucasian grape vodka out of their travelling supplies. He gulped down a big glassful, said his prayers before the folding travelling icon, covered himself with his overcoat and started snoring such a time that none of the Englishmen in the whole house could get any sleep.

He thought, 'Wait until the morning light; it's always wiser than the night.'

2

The next day the Emperor and Platov went to the museums. The Emperor took none of his other Russians with him, because the carriage they gave him was only a two-sitter.

They came to a great big building, with an entrance beyond description, corridors beyond measure, and one room after another, until at last they came into the biggest hall of all, with tremendulous estuaries, and right in the middle, under a canoply, stood the Apollo Velvet Ear.

The Emperor glanced around sideways at Platov to see what he was looking at and whether he was very much amazed; but Platov was walking along with his eyes looking down at the ground as if he didn't see anything, and he was only winding his moustaches into rings.

The Englishmen started at once to show off all sorts of marvels and explain how everything in them was fitted together with everything else for military circumstances. There were nautical whether-meters, gamblehair coats for the infantry and waterproof rein coats for the cavalry. The Emperor was glad to see all this, and he thought everything looked very good; but Platov held his impatience and said it all didn't mean a thing for him.

The Emperor said, 'How is that possible? How can you be so unfeeling? Doesn't anything at all impress you here?'

And Platov replied, 'Just one thing impresses me here: my Don River boys fought without all this and drove out old Bony Part.'

The Emperor said, 'That's just prejudunce.'

Platov answered, 'I don't know what to call it, but I ain't allowed to argue so I'll keep quiet.'

The Englishmen, seeing this exchange between the Emperor, at once took him up to the statue of Apollo Velvet Ear itself and took a Mortimer rifle out of one hand and a pistol out of the other.

'Here's the kind of production we've got,' they said, and they handed him the rifle.

The Emperor looked calmly at the Mortimer rifle, because he had some like it at home in his Summer Palace, and then they handed him the pistol and said, 'This is a pistol of unknown and inimitable workmanship. Our admiral snatched it off the belt of a robber chieftain at Candelabria.'

The Emperor fastened his eyes on the pistol and couldn't get enough of looking at it.

He oh-ed and ah-ed something awful.

'Oh! Oh! Oh!' he says. 'What do you know about that! How is it possible to do such fine work!' And he turned to Platov and said to him in Russian: 'Now if only I had just one craftsman like that in Russia I would be a very happy man; I'd be so proud I would make a nobleman of him on the spot.'

At these words Platov stuck his right hand into his big wide trousers and pulled out a gunsmith's screwdriver. The Englishmen said, 'This won't come open,' but Platov, paying no attention to them, started tinkering with the gunlock. He turned it once, he turned it twice – and the gun opened up. Platov showed the Emperor the trigger, and right there in the crook was a Russian inscription: *Ivan Moskvin in Tula Town.*

The Englishmen were amazed and nudged each other: 'Uh-oh!' they said. 'We slipped up that time.'

But the Emperor said sadly to Platov, 'Why did you have to embarrass them so much? Let's go.'

They got into their two-sitter again and started off, and the Emperor went to a ball that evening, but Platov downed a still bigger glass of grape vodka and slept the sound sleep of the Cossacks.

He had been glad to put the Englishmen to rout and attract contention to the Tula gunsmith, but he had been put out as well: why did the Emperor have to feel sorry for the Englishmen in a case like this?

'Why did the Emperor feel bad about it?' thought Platov. 'I can't figure it out at all.' And in this consideration he got up twice, crossed himself, and drank vodka until at last he forced himself into a sound sleep.

At that same time the Englishmen were not asleep either, because their heads were spinning, too. While the Emperor was having a good time at the ball, they cooked up such a new marvel for him that they completely knocked the imagination out of Platov.

3

The next day, when Platov reported to the Emperor to say good morning, he told Platov, 'Have the two-sitter carriage hitched up, and let's go to look at some more museums.'

Platov even made bold to ask the Emperor whether they hadn't looked at enough outlandish products, and wouldn't it be better to get ready to go back to Russia, but the Emperor said, 'No, I wish to see still other novelties here; they have boasted to me about how they make sugar of the very highest quality.'

They started off.

The Englishmen showed everything to the Emperor – just how many different highest qualities they had – and

Platov looked and looked, and then suddenly he said, 'But won't you show us your factories where you make Molvo sugar?'

The Englishmen didn't know what 'Molvo' was. They whispered back and forth to each other, winked back and forth to each other, and repeated to each other, 'Molvo, Molvo,' but they couldn't understand what kind of sugar that was that we made in our country, and they had to admit that they had all kinds of sugar – but no 'Molvo'.

Platov said, 'Well, then, you haven't got anything to brag about. Come to our country and we'll fill you full of tea with genuwine Molvo sugar from Bobrinsky's factory.'

But the Emperor tugged him by the sleeve and said quietly: 'Now, please don't go and spoil my politics.'

Then the Englishmen invited the Emperor to their very latest museum, where they had brought together mineral stones and nymphusorias from all over the world, beginning with the most enormous Egyptian hobble lists and coming down to the hide-bound flea, which you can't see with your eyes but can only feel when he bites you between your hide and your body.

The Emperor set out.

They looked at the hobble lists and all kinds of stuffed animals, and then came out and Platov thought to himself, 'There now, thank the Lord, everything is turning out all right: the Emperor hasn't marvelled at anything.'

But as soon as they got to the very last room, there were workmen standing around in everyday jackets and aprons holding a tray that had nothing on it.

Then the Emperor really did marvel because they offered him an empty tray.

'What does this mean?' he asked, and the English craftsmen replied, 'This is our humble offering to your Highness.'

'But what *is* it?'

'Well,' they said, 'does your Highness kindly see this little speck?'

The Emperor took a look and saw that there really was the tiniest little speck lying on the tray.

The workmen said, 'Be so kind as to spit on your finger and pick it up and put it on your hand.'

'What good is that speck to me?'

'That,' they answered, 'is not a speck but a nymphusoria.'

'Is it alive?'

'No, sir,' they answered, 'it's not alive. We made it in the shape of a flea out of pure English steel, and inside it is a motor and a spring. Be so kind as to wind it up with the key: then it will do a little *dansez*.'

The Emperor got curious and asked, 'But where is the key?'

The Englishmen replied, 'Here is the key, right in front of your eyes.'

'Then why can't I see it?' asked the Emperor.

'Because,' they said, 'you have to blow it up in a nitroscope.'

A nitroscope was brought in, and the Emperor saw that a little key really was lying on the tray beside the flea.

'Be so kind as to take it in your hand,' they said. 'There's a hole in its belly for the key, and the key will take seven turns. Then it will start its *dansez*.'

The Emperor could barely pick up the key and barely hold it in his fingers. He took hold of the flea with his other hand and hadn't hardly stuck the key in before he felt the whiskers move, and then the legs started working, and at last it suddenly jumped up and in one bound did a straight *dansez* and two fairiations to one side and then to the other, and danced like that through a whole cod drill in three fairiations.

The Emperor gave orders on the spot to give a million to the Englishmen in any kind of money they wanted – either in silver five-kopek coins, if they wished, or else in small bills.

The Englishmen asked for it in silver, because they couldn't make heads or tails out of paper money, and then right off they pulled another one of their shifty tricks: they handed over the flea as a gift, but they hadn't brought any case for it. Without a case you couldn't keep either the flea or the key, because they would get lost and thrown out with the trash. But they had made a case out of a diamond in the shape of a nut, with a hole dug out of the middle for the flea. They didn't make a gift of this, because they said the case was government property, and they are very strict over there about government property, even for the Emperor – you can't give it away.

Platov was about to get hot under the collar, and he said, 'What's the idea of all this swindle! They gave us a gift and they got a million for it, and still that isn't enough! The case,' he says, 'always goes with such things as these.'

But the Emperor said, 'Leave off, please, this isn't your affair – don't go and spoil my politics. They have their own customs.' And he asked, 'How much does that nut cost that the flea fits into?'

The Englishmen reckoned that would be five thousand more.

Emperor Aleksandr said, 'Pay them,' and put the flea in that nut himself, and the key along with it, and so as not to lose the nut he put it into his gold snuffbox, and he ordered the snuffbox put into his little travelling casket, which was all covered with the mother of pearl and fishbones. The Emperor dismissed the English workmen with honour and said to them, 'You are the finest workmen in the whole world, and my men can't do anything compared to you.'

They were very pleased with this, and Platov could say nothing against the words of his Emperor. Only he took the nitroscope and slipped it in his pocket without saying anything, because 'it goes with it,' he says, 'and you've taken a lot of money from us already.'

The Emperor knew nothing about that till he got to Russia. They left right away, because military affairs had filled the Emperor with melancholy and he wanted to go to spiritual confession before Father Fedot in Taganrog. On the way he and Platov had a mighty unpleasant conversation, because they had entirely different ideas in their heads: the Emperor thought nobody could come up to the Englishmen in art, and Platov begged to report that our people could make anything once they got a good look at it, only they didn't have any useful training. And he pointed out to the Emperor that the English workmen have completely different rules of life, science and production for everything, and every man among them has all the absolute circumstances before him, and for that reason he has a completely different meaning.

The Emperor would not listen very long to that, and when Platov saw this he didn't insist. So they rode along in silence, only Platov would get out at every station and in his aggravation he would drink up a big glass of vodka, eat a little salt mutton, light up his enormous pipe, which was big enough to hold a whole pound of Zhukov tobacco, and then take his seat and sit without saying a word beside the Tsar in the carriage. The Emperor would look off in one direction, and Platov would stick his chibouk out the other window and smoke into the wind. This was how they rode all the way to Petersburg, and when the Emperor went on to see Father Fedot he didn't take Platov at all.

'You,' he said, 'are intemperate in spiritual conversation, and you smoke so much that my head is full of soot from your pipe.'

Platov felt insulted and he lay down at home on his bed of ire, and just kept on lying there, smoking his Zhukov tobacco without intercession.

4

The marvellous flea of blue English steel remained in Aleksandr the First's little fishbone casket until he died in Taganrog, after turning it over to Father Fedot to pass on to the Empress when she calmed down. Empress Elizabeth Alexeyevna looked at the flea's fairiations and smiled, but she didn't take an interest in it.

'My affairs now,' she said, 'are widow's affairs, and no amusements can win my attention,' and when she got back to Petersburg she handed over this wonder with all her other valuables as an inheritance for the new emperor.

In the beginning Tsar Nicholas the First also paid no attention to the flea, because there was trouble at the time he got up on the throne, but after that one day he started looking through the little casket that had come down to him from his brother, and he took out the snuffbox, and out of the snuffbox he took the diamond nut, and in it he found the steel flea, which had not been wound up in a long time and for that reason was not moving, but lay there quietly like it was numb.

The Emperor looked at it in amazement.

'What can this trifle be, and to what purpose did my brother preserve it in this way?'

The courtiers wanted to throw it out, but the Emperor said, 'No, this must mean something.'

They called a druggist from the pharmacy effacing the Anichkin Bridge, who weighed poisons in the very finest scales. They showed it to him, and he took the flea and put it on his tongue and said, 'I feel something cold, like strong metal.' And then he mashed it a little with his teeth and announced, 'Say what you please, but this is not a genuine flea but a nymphusoria, and it is made of metal, and the work is not ours – not Russian.'

The Emperor ordered that inquiries should be made at once about where it had come from and what it signified.

They plunged into an examination of the records and the lists, but nothing was written in the records. They began asking this one and that, but nobody knew anything. By good luck, though, Platov the Don Cossack was still alive and even still lying on his bed of ire and smoking his pipe. As soon as he heard about all that disturbance at the Court, he rose up from his bed, threw down his pipe and reported to the Emperor with all his decorations. The Emperor said, 'What need have you of me, courageous old man?'

And Platov answered, 'I need nothing for myself, Your Majesty, since I eat and drink all I want and I'm satisfied with everything. But,' he says, 'I have come to report about that nymphusoria they found. This is the way it was,' he says, 'this is how it happened right before my eyes in England, and right here beside it is the key, and I've got their own nitroscope, that you can use to blow it up and look at it, and with this key you can wind up the nymphusoria through its belly, and it will hop around in any space you want and do fairiations to each side.'

They wound it up, it began to jump, and Platov said, 'You're right, Your Majesty,' he says, 'that the work is mighty fine and interesting, only it's not right for us to marvel at it with nothing but the rapture of our feelings. It ought to be submitted for Russian inspection at Tula or Sesterbek (at that time Sestroretsk was still called Sesterbek), to see whether our craftsmen can't outdo it, so that the Englishmen won't keep lording it over us Russians.'

Emperor Nicholas had great confidence in his Russian men and didn't like to yield to any foreigner, and so he answered Platov, 'You speak well, courageous old man, and I charge you with the task of proving this matter. With all my cares I do not need this little box. You take it with you, and lie no more on your bed of ire, but go to the silent Don, and strike up intimidating conversations there with my Don people about their life and devotion and what is pleasing to them. And when you go through

Tula, show this nymphusoria to my Tula craftsmen, that they may ponder over it. Tell them from me that my brother marvelled at this thing, and he praised above all others the foreigners who made this nymphusoria, but I place my hope in my own people, that they are surpassed by no one. They will heed my word and will do something.'

5

Platov took the steel flea, and when he went through Tula toward the Don, he showed it to the Tula gunsmiths and passed the Emperor's words on to them and then asked, 'Now what can we do about it, Orthodox brethren?'

The gunsmiths replied, 'Worthy old man we feel the gracious word of the Emperor, and we never can forget it, because he puts his hope in his own people, but what we can do about it in this here case we can't say in just one minute, because the English nation ain't stupid either; they're even sort of cunning, and their art is full of horse sense. We mustn't go out after them till we've pondered about it and got God's blessing. Now, if you have confidence in us like the Emperor, then journey hence to your home upon the silent Don, and leave us this here little flea just like it is, in its case and in the golden snuffbox of the Tsar. Make yourself merry along the Don and heal the wounds you have suffered for our

15

fatherland, and when you return through Tula, tarry and send for us: by that time, God willing, it may be that we'll have something thunk up.'

Platov was not completely satisfied because the Tula workmen demanded so much time and didn't talk very clearly about just what they hoped to make. He asked them this way and that, and using his Don Cossack cunning he talked with them in every sort of way, but the Tula men were no less cunning than he was, because they already had thought up such a plan that they couldn't really hope even Platov would believe them, and they wanted to carry out their bold idea right away and then hand it over.

They said, 'Even we ourselves don't know yet what we'll do, but we'll only rest our faith in God and trust that the Tsar's word won't be put to shame through our doings.'

Platov kept twisting and turning this way and that, and so did the men from Tula.

Platov wriggled and wriggled till he saw that he couldn't outwriggle a Tula man, and then he handed over the snuffbox with the nymphusoria and said, 'Well, there's nothing to do. Let it be your way,' he says. 'I know you – what kind you are. Still, there's nothing to do – I believe you. Only take care and don't try to swap diamonds on me, and don't spoil the fine English workmanship, and don't fool around very long, because I travel fast. Two weeks won't go by before I return again from the silent

Don to Petersburg. At that time see to it that I have something to show the Emperor.'

The gunsmiths reassured him completely, 'We ain't
going to harm the fine workmanship,' they said, 'and we
won't change diamonds on you, and two weeks are
enough time for us, and by the time you come back you
will have *something* worthy to be shown to his Imperial
Splendour.'

But exactly *what* it was they just wouldn't say.

6

Platov departed from Tula; and three of the gunsmiths,
the most skilful of them all – one of them a cross-eyed
left-handed man with a birthmark on his cheek and bald
spots on his temples where the hair had been pulled out
when he was an apprentice – these three bade farewell to
their fellow workmen and their families, and without saying anything to anybody they took their bags, put what
food they needed into them, and disappeared from town.

The only thing anybody noticed was that they didn't go
out through the Moscow gate, but through the one on the
other side, in the direction of Kiev, and people thought
they had gone to Kiev to bow down before the saints rest-
ing there in peace or to take counsel with some of the holy
men still alive there, who were always available in abun-
dance in Kiev.

But this was only close to the truth and not the truth itself. Neither time nor distance allowed the Tula craftsmen in three weeks to walk to Kiev and then on top of that to make something that would put the English nation to shame. They might have done better to go and pray in Moscow, which was only 'twice fifty miles away', and a good many holy saints rest in peace there too. In the other direction too it was 'twice fifty miles' to Oryol and then another good three hundred from Oryol to Kiev. You won't get over that much ground in a hurry, and even when you've done it you won't get rested in a hurry: for a long time your feet will feel as numb as glass and your hands will tremble.

Some people even thought the craftsmen had bragged a little too much to Platov and then after they thought it over had got scared and run away for good, taking along the Tsar's gold snuffbox, and the diamond, and the English steel flea in its case that had brought them all the trouble.

However, this supposition too was completely unfounded, and was unworthy of the clever men on whom the hope of the nation now rested.

7

The inhabitants of Tula, who are intelligent people and knowledgeable about metal work, are also well known as the finest experts in religion. Their fame in this connection has spread all over their native land and has even reached Mount Athos: they are not only masters at singing their fancy trills; they also know how to paint the picture *Evening Bells*, and if any of them dedicate themselves to greater service and enter monastic life, they become famous as the best managers of monastery household affairs, and they make the most capable collectors of alms. On holy Mount Athos everybody knows that the Tula inhabitants are a most remunerative people, and if it wasn't for them, most likely the dark corners of Russia would not see very many holy relics from the distant East, and Mount Athos would be deprived of many useful contributions from Russian generosity and piety. Today the 'Tula men of Mount Athos' carry holy relics all over our native land and skilfully collect contributions even where there is nothing to collect. The Tula man is full of churchly piety and is highly practical in this matter, and so the three master craftsmen who took it on themselves to uphold Platov, and with him all Russia, made no mistake when they headed south instead of towards Moscow. They didn't go to Kiev at all but to Mtsensk, to the district town of Oryol Province in which there stands the ancient 'stone-graven' icon of Saint Nicholas, which was brought here in the most ancient times along the river Zusha on a large cross, likewise made of stone. This icon is 'awesome and most terrible' in appearance. The sainted archbishop of Myra in Lycia is represented on it full-length, clothed all over in silver-gilt clothing, swarthy of face and holding a temple in one hand and the sword of 'Military Conquest' in the other. It was just this 'Conquest' that held the meaning of the whole thing: Saint Nicholas in general and 'Nicholas of Mtsensk' in particular was the patron saint of commerce and warfare, and so the Tula gunsmiths went to make their bows to him. They held their prayer service right in front of the icon, and then in front of the stone cross, and finally, returning home by night and saying nothing to anybody, they set about their work in awful secrecy. All three of them got together in Lefty's house; they locked the doors, boarded up the windows, lighted a lamp before the icon of Saint Nicholas and started to work.

One day, two days, three days they sat without going out anywhere, all of them tapping away with their hammers. They were making something, but what it was they were making nobody knew.

Everyone was curious, but nobody could find out a thing, because the workmen said nothing and never stuck their noses outside. All sorts of people would go up to the little house and knock on the door with all sorts of excuses, to ask for fire or borrow some salt, but the three experts would not open up for any kind of request. Even how they got food nobody knew. People tried to scare them, and pretended that the house next door was on fire to see whether they wouldn't run out in fright and give away the secret of what they were making, but nothing could take in those shrewd workmen. Lefty stuck his head out only once and shouted, 'Go ahead and burn up; we ain't got time,' and then he drew in his plucked head, banged the shutters tight and got to work again. Through the tiny cracks people could only see the glitter of a light and hear the ringing blows of tiny hammers tapping on anvils.

In a word, the whole thing was handled in such awful secrecy that there was no way to find out anything about it, and it lasted right up to the return of the Cossack Platov from the silent Don on his way to the Emperor, and during all that time the craftsmen saw nobody and said nothing.

8

Platov travelled in great haste and ceremony: he himself sat in the carriage, and on the coach-boxes two Cossack scurriers holding whips sat on each side of the driver and poured it on him unmercifully so as to make him hurry. If either one of the Cossacks dozed off, Platov would give him a kick from inside the carriage, and they would tear along even more wildly. These measures worked so well that there was no holding back the horses at a single station anywhere; they would always gallop on a hundred paces past the halting-place. Then the Cossack would work on the driver once more in the opposite direction, and they would go back to the entrance.

That was the way they rolled into Tula: there too at first they flew a hundred paces beyond the Moscow gate, and then the Cossack worked on the driver with his whip in the opposite direction, and at the entrance they started hitching up fresh horses. Platov didn't get out of the carriage, but only told his scurrier to go as fast as possible and get the craftsmen he had left the flea with.

One scurrier dashed off to get them to come as fast as possible and bring him the work that was to put the Englishmen to shame, and that scurrier had run only a short distance when Platov sent first one and then another after him so as to speed things up.

He sent off all his scurriers and then began dispatching ordinary people from the curious crowd, and in impatience he even stuck his own legs out of the carriage and was about to start running impatiently himself, and he gritted his teeth because they were all so slow in coming into sight.

In those days everything had to be done just right and very fast, so as not to lose a minute that might be useful to Russia.

9

At that very moment the Tula craftsmen who were making the marvellous thing had finished their work. The scurriers ran up to them puffing and blowing, and the ordinary people from the curious crowd – well, they didn't even get there at all, because their legs, being out of practice, scattered and fell all along the way, and then in terror, for fear they might catch sight of Platov, they lit out for home and hid wherever they could.

As soon as the scurriers ran up, they gave a shout, and when they saw that nobody opened up, they jerked at the bolts on the shutters, but the bolts were so strong they wouldn't give at all; they pulled at the doors, but the doors were fastened from the inside with heavy oak bars. Then the scurriers picked up a beam from the street and stuck it under the eave of the roof the way firemen do, and in one blow they prized the whole roof off the hut. But as soon as they got the roof off, they themselves keeled over, because the workmen with their unceaseless labour in their crowded little shanty had expired so much that a man who wasn't used to it, coming right in when the wind was dead, instinkly choked.

The messengers cried out, 'What are you doing, you so-and-so's, you swine? What do you mean by knocking us over with that expiration? Or ain't you got any fear of God left in you?'

And they answered, 'Just a minute, we're driving in the last nail, and as soon as we hammer it down we'll bring out our work.'

The messengers said, 'He'll eat us alive before then and won't even leave our souls for the funeral.'

But the craftsmen answered, 'He won't have time to

gobble you up, because we drove the last nail in while you were standing there talking. Run and tell him we're bringing it right now.'

The scurriers dashed off, but their hearts weren't in it, because they thought the craftsmen might fool them, and for that reason they ran and ran, but kept looking back. But the craftsmen were coming along behind them, and they had hurried so fast they hadn't even got dressed quite the way they ought for a meeting with an important person, and while they ran they were still fastening the hooks of their kaftans. Two of them had nothing in their hands, but the third one, Lefty, had the Tsar's jewel casket wrapped in a green cloth cover with the English steel flea inside.

## 10

The scurriers ran up to Platov and said, 'Here they are in person!'

Platov barked at the craftsmen, 'Is it ready?'

'It's all ready,' they answered.

'Give it here.'

They handed it over.

The carriage was already hitched up, and the driver and postillion were in their places. The Cossacks at once took their seats beside the driver and raised their whips over his head and held them brandished there.

Platov snatched off the green cover, opened the little casket, took the gold snuffbox out of its padding and the diamond nut out of the snuffbox. He saw the English flea lying there just the way it had before, and apart from it nothing else was there.

Platov said, 'What's the meaning of this? Where is your work that you wanted to console the Emperor with?'

The gunsmiths answered, 'Our work is right there.'

Platov asked, 'What kind of work?'

The gunsmiths answered, 'What's the use of explaining? Everything is right there in front of your eyes. Just take a look at it.'

Platov squared his shoulders and shouted, 'Where's the key to the flea?'

'Why, it's right here,' they answered. 'Where the flea is, there the key is – in the same nut.'

Platov tried to take hold of the key, but his fingers were too stubby. He grabbed and grabbed but couldn't catch either the flea or the key to its bellyworks, and suddenly he burst out and started swearing with colourful Cossack words.

He shouted, 'You scoundrels, you've done nothing at all, and on top of it you've probably ruined the whole thing! I'll take off your heads!'

But the Tula men answered him, 'There ain't no use insulting us. From you, as the Emperor's messenger, we've got to put up with all insults, but just because you wouldn't trust us and thought we were the kind that would even cheat the Emperor hisself, we ain't going to tell you the secret of our work now; just be so kind as to take it to the Emperor, and he'll see what sort of men he's got in us, and whether we've done anything to make him ashamed of us.'

Platov shouted, 'You're lying, you scoundrels, and I won't let you get away from me like that. One of you will go with me to Petersburg, and there I'll get out of him what kind of scullduggery you've been up to.'

And with this he reached out, grabbed the cross-eyed Lefty by the collar with his stubby fingers, so that all the hooks flew off his kazakin shirt, and pitched him into the carriage at his feet.

'Lie there like a puddle,' he said, 'till we get to Petersburg. You'll answer to me for all of them. And you,' he said to the scurriers, 'get a move on! Look sharp now, and see to it that I'm in Petersburg at the Emperor's the day after tomorrow!'

The craftsmen stuck their necks out for their comrade and asked how he could be taken away from them like that without his grasp port. Then he would have no way to get back! But instead of answering them Platov just showed them his fist – a frightful one, all knotty and hacked apart and somehow grown back together again – and waving it in front of them he said, 'There's a grasp port for you!'

And he said to his Cossacks, 'Let's go, boys!'

His Cossacks, drivers and steeds all started working at

once and they whisked Lefty away without his grasp port, and two days later, just as Platov had ordered, they rolled up to the Emperor's palace, arriving at such a properly furious gallop that they drove right past the columns.

Platov stood up, hooked on his decorations and went in to the Emperor, telling his Cossack scurriers to keep watch at the entrance over cross-eyed Lefty.

## 11

Platov was afraid to report to the Emperor in person, because it was awful how noticeable and memorable Tsar Nicholas was – he never forgot anything. Platov knew he was bound to ask him about the flea. And even though he was afraid of no enemy on earth, right here he got cold feet: he carried the little casket into the palace and very quietly laid it down in the hall behind the stove. With the box hidden he presented himself to the Emperor in his office and quickly began reporting on the intimidating conversations he'd had with the Cossacks on the silent Don. He figured he would try to keep the Emperor busy with this. Then if the Emperor remembered and started talking about the flea, he would have to hand it over and answer, but if the Emperor didn't say anything about it, he could just keep quiet. He would tell the Emperor's servant to hide the little casket and lock up Lefty in a fortress cell so as to keep him handy in case he might be needed.

But Emperor Nicholas forgot about nothing, and Platov had barely finished about the intimidating conversations when he asked at once, 'And how about it – how did my Tula craftsmen justify themselves against the English nymphusoria?'

Platov answered the way the matter looked to him.

'Your Majesty,' he says, 'the nymphusoria is still lying in that same space, and I have brought it back, but the Tula craftsmen couldn't make anything more marvellous.'

The Emperor replied, 'You are a courageous old man, but what you report to me cannot be so.'

Platov tried to convince him and told him how the whole thing had happened, and when he got to the part where the Tula workmen asked him to show the flea to the Emperor, Tsar Nicholas slapped him on the back and said, 'Give it here. I know my men won't let me down. Something has been done here that is past all understanding.'

12

They brought the little casket out from behind the stove, they took the cloth cover off, they opened the gold snuff-box and the diamond nut – and there the flea was, lying just the way it had before.

The Emperor took a look and said, 'What a misfortune!' But his faith in his Russian craftsmen didn't slacken, and he sent for his favourite daughter Aleksandra and commanded her, 'You have slender fingers: hasten, take that little key and wind up the bellyworks of that nymphusoria.'

The princess began to wind it up, and the flea at once started wiggling its whiskers, but it didn't move its feet. Aleksandra pulled on the whole works, but still the nymphusoria wouldn't do a single *dansez* or fairiation, the way it used to.

Platov turned green all over and shouted, 'Oh those rascally dogs! Now I understand why they wouldn't tell me anything. It's lucky I brought one of their blockheads along with me.'

With these words he ran out to the entrance, grabbed Lefty by the hair, and began to swing him back and forth so hard that tufts of it started flying. When Platov had stopped beating him, Lefty straightened himself out and said, 'That's the way all my hair got pulled out while I was an apprentice. I don't know what need there is now to go through all that again.'

'That's because I'd counted on you and vouched for you,' said Platov, 'and then you went and spoiled that rarity.'

Lefty answered, 'We're mighty glad you vouched for us, and as for spoiling – we didn't spoil nothing. Just blow it up in your strongest nitroscope and take a look.'

Platov ran back to tell them about the nitroscope, but

to Lefty he only warned, 'I'll give you this-that-and-the-other even yet.'

He ordered the scurriers to twist Lefty's arms even harder behind his back, and he himself went up the steps, puffing and blowing and repeating the prayer, 'Blessed Tsar's Most Blessed Mother, immaculate and pure,' and so on, as needed. And the courtiers who were standing on the steps all turned their backs on him. They thought, 'Platov is done for now, and he'll soon be chased out of the palace,' because they couldn't stand him on account of his bravery.

## 13

As soon as Platov reported Lefty's words to the Emperor, he said full of joy, 'I know my Russian men will not let me down.' And he ordered the nitroscope to be brought forward on a pillow.

The nitroscope was brought forward that very minute, and the Emperor took the flea and laid it under the glass, first on its belly, then on its side and then on its back. In a word, it was turned in every direction, but nothing could be seen. Still the Emperor didn't lose faith. He only said, 'Bring hither at once that gunsmith who is waiting below.'

Platov reported, 'They'd have to dress him up. He's still

got the clothes on he was caught in, and now he's in bad shape.'

But the Emperor replied, 'Never mind; bring him in just as he is.'

Platov said, 'Come in here, now, you so-and-so, and answer to the Emperor before his eyes.'

Lefty replied, 'Why, sure, I'll go like this and I'll answer.'

He went like he was: in ragged boots, with one trouser-leg tucked in and the other dangling, with an old jacket that wouldn't fasten because the hooks were lost, and with the collar that was torn; but it didn't matter – he wasn't embarrassed.

'What of it?' he thought. 'If the Emperor wants to see me, I've got to go, and if I ain't got a grasp port, it ain't my fault, and I'll tell him how it happened.'

As soon as Lefty came in and bowed, the Emperor said to him, 'What does this mean, my good man? We have looked this way and that and have blown it up in the nitroscope and we still can't find anything remarkable.'

Lefty answered, 'Did Your Majesty be so kind as to look at it the right way?'

The nobles motioned to him to tell him that was not the way to talk, but he didn't understand how to talk courtier language – with flattery or cunning – and he kept on talking simply.

The Emperor said to them, 'Stop making things complicated for him; let him answer as he knows how.'

And then he explained to Lefty, 'This is the way we laid it,' he says. And he put the flea under the nitroscope. 'Look at it yourself,' he says. 'You can't see a thing.'

Lefty answered, 'You can't see nothing that way, Your Majesty, because our work is a lot too secret for that size.'

The Emperor asked, 'Then how *do* we manage it?'

'You have to put just one of its feet in detail under the whole nitroscope, and look one at a time at each foot it walks on.'

'Goodness Gracious,' said the Emperor. 'That's powerfully small.'

'But what else can you do,' answered Lefty, 'if that's the only way you can get a look at our work? Then you can see the whole amazement.'

They laid it down the way Lefty said and as soon as the Emperor looked in the upper glass, he beamed all over. He grabbed Lefty just the way he was – dirty, dusty, unwashed – and put his arms around him and kissed him on the cheek, and then he turned to all the courtiers and said, 'You see, I knew better than everybody that my Russians would not let me down. Just look: why, the rascals have taken the English flea and nailed flea-shoes on its feet!'

14

They all came up to look: all the flea's feet really were shod with genuine flea-shoes, and Lefty reported that this was not the only marvel.

'If you had a better nitroscope,' he said, 'one that would blow it up five million times, then you could be so kind as to see that a craftsman's name was put on each shoe, so as to show which Russian gunsmith made that shoe.'

'Is your name there too?' asked the Emperor.

'No, sir,' answered Lefty. 'Mine is the only one that ain't.'

'Why isn't it?'

'Because I did smaller work than these flea-shoes,' he said. 'I made the nails the shoes were fastened on with, and they are too small for any nitroscope to blow them up.'

The Emperor asked, 'But where is your nitroscope, which you used to produce this marvel?'

Lefty answered, 'We are poor people – too poor to own a nitroscope, so we just sharpened our eyes.'

Seeing that Lefty's business had turned out well, the other courtiers began to kiss him and Platov gave him a hundred roubles and said, 'Forgive me, brother, for dragging you around by the hair.'

Lefty answered, 'God will forgive you – it ain't the first time that kind of snow has fallen on my head.'

He would say no more – and he didn't even have time to say more, because the Emperor ordered the iron-shod nymphusoria to be packed up and sent back at once to England, as a sort of gift, to make them understand that it wasn't any marvel to us. And the Emperor ordered the flea to be carried by a special courier who was learned in all languages, and ordered the left-handed smith to go with him so that he himself could show their work to the Englishmen and show them what kind of craftsmen we have in Tula.

Platov made the sign of the Cross over him.

'Blessings be upon you,' he said. 'I'll send you some of my own grape vodka for the journey. Don't drink too little and don't drink too much – drink middlesome.'

And so he did – he sent it.

Count Nestlebroad gave orders to wash Lefty in the Tula Public Baths, cut his hair in a barber shop, and deck him out in the full-dress coat of a singer in the royal choir, so that he would look like he had some kind of paid government rank.

As soon as they had worked him over this way, they filled him with tea and Platov's grape vodka, drew up his belt as tight as possible so that his guts wouldn't shake, and sent him off to London. That is when foreign sights started happening to Lefty.

15

The courier travelled powerfully fast with Lefty, so that they didn't stop to rest anywhere between Petersburg and London, but only drew their belts another notch tighter at every station, so that their guts wouldn't get mixed up with their lungs; but since Lefty on Platov's orders was allotted as much government vodka as he wanted after he had been presented to the Emperor, he kept up his strength on this alone, without eating anything, and he sang Russian songs all the way through Europe – only adding a refrain of foreign words,

> *Aye loolee*
> *Say tray Joe Lee.*

As soon as the courier got him to London, he reported to the proper authorities and handed over the box, and then put Lefty down in a hotel room; but there he soon began to get restless, and besides, he was hungry. He knocked on the door and pointed to his mouth when the servant came, and the servant took him right off to the feeding room.

Here Lefty sat down at a table and waited. He didn't know how to ask for anything in English. But then he figured it out, again he just tapped on the table with his finger and pointed to his mouth; the Englishmen guessed what he meant and served him, only they didn't always bring what he wanted. But he wouldn't take anything that didn't suit him. They brought him their kind of hot glum pudding in flames. He said, 'I don't see how anybody can eat that,' and he wouldn't take a bite. They exchanged it for him and brought him something else to eat. He wouldn't drink their vodka, either, because it was green – like they had flavoured it with sulphuric acid. He picked out the plainest stuff they had, and waited in the cool with his canteen for the courier.

And the people the courier had handed the nymphusoria over to looked at it that very minute through their strongest nitroscope and sent a description right off to a calumnist on the *Daily Telegraft*, so that he could tell everybody about it the very next day.

'And as for that craftsman,' they said, 'we want to see him at once.' The courier took them to the hotel room and from there to the feeding room, where our Lefty had begun to glow very decently, and said, 'There he is.'

The Englishmen slapped Lefty on the back right away and took him by the hands just like their own equal. 'Comrade,' they said, 'comrade, you're a good craftsman. We'll talk to you afterwards when there is time, but now we want to drink to your prosperity.'

They ordered a lot of wine and gave Lefty the first glass, but out of politeness he wouldn't be the first to drink. He thought, 'Maybe you're so aggravated you want to poison me.'

'No,' he said, 'that's not the way to do it. Even with a Polish thirst, you have to let the host drink first. You yourselves drink on ahead.'

The Englishmen tasted all their wines in front of him and then started filling his glass. He stood up, crossed himself with his left hand, and drank to the health of them all.

They noticed that he had crossed himself with his left hand, and they asked the courier, 'What is he – a Lutheranian or a Protesterian?'

The courier answered, 'He's not either a Lutheranian or a Protestarian; he belongs to the Russian faith.'

'But why does he cross himself with his left hand?'

The courier replied, 'He's a left-handed man, and he does everything with his left hand.'

The Englishmen marvelled even more and started pumping both Lefty and the courier full of wine, and kept on this way for three whole days, and then they said, 'Now that's enough.' They symphonied some water out of a bottle with impressed air, and when they were refreshed all over they started asking Lefty all about where had he studied, and what had he studied, and how far had he gone in arithmetic.

Lefty answered, 'Our learning is simple – according to the Psalter and the *Dream-Book*. We don't know no arithmetic at all.'

The Englishmen looked at each other and said, 'That's amazing.'

And Lefty answered, 'It's that way all over in our country.'

'But what sort of book is that in Russia,' they asked, 'that dream-book?'

'That book,' he said, 'refers to if King David didn't reveal some fortune-telling clearly in the Psalter, then you can get some extra fortunes out of the *Dream-Book*.'

They said, 'That's too bad. It would be better if you at least knew the four rules of addition; that would be a lot more utilifying to you than your whole *Dream-Book*. Then you would be able to understand that every machine has its balance of forces. As it is, even though you are mighty skilful with your hands, you didn't realize that such a little machine as the one in the nymphusoria was calcu-lated for the most accurate exactness, and it can't carry the flea-shoes. That's why the nymphusoria won't jump or dance any *dansez*.'

Lefty agreed, 'About that there ain't no argument,' he said. 'We didn't get very far in book-learning, but only faithfully serve our fatherland.'

And the Englishmen said to him, 'Stay here with us; we'll give you a big education and you'll turn out to be a superbluous craftsman.'

But Lefty wouldn't agree. 'I've got my parents at home,' he said.

The Englishmen offered to send his parents money, but Lefty wouldn't take it.

'We are devoted to our country,' he said, 'and my

daddy's an old man and my mother's an old woman, and they're used to going to church in their own parish, and it would be mighty lonely here for me all by myself, because I'm still a bachelor by calling.'

'You'll get used to it,' they said. 'You'll accept our laws, and we'll get you married.'

'That can never be,' answered Lefty.

'Why not?'

'Because,' he answered, 'our Russian faith is the rightest one, and the way our forefathers believed is just the way their dissentants have to believe.'

'You don't know our faith,' said the Englishmen. 'We've got the same Christian law and hold to the same Gospel.'

'It's true,' said Lefty, 'that everybody's got the same Gospel, but our books are thicker than yours, and our faith is fuller.'

'How can you judge that way?'

'We've got all the evident proofs of it,' he answered.

'What kind?'

'Why, we've got God-wondering icons and prism-working relics, and you ain't got nothing – except for Sunday you ain't even got any special holidays. And the second reason is that even if I was married in the law to an English girl it would be confusing to live with her.'

'How's that?' they asked. 'Don't turn up your nose at our girls – they too dress neatly and they're good housekeepers.'

But Lefty said, 'I don't know them.'

The Englishmen replied, 'That's no problem – you'll get to know them. We'll fix up a roundy-view for you.'

Lefty started blushing. 'What's the use of stringing the girls along for no reason?' he said, and he wouldn't budge. 'That's something for fine gentlemen. It wouldn't suit us. And if they found out about it at home, in Tula, they'd make fun of me something awful.'

The Englishmen got curious, 'Then suppose we did it without a roundy-view,' they said. 'How do you manage in your country so as to make a favourable choice?'

Lefty explained our way to them. 'In our country,' he said, 'when a man wants to reveal a circumstantial intention in regard to a girl, he sends over a conversational woman, and when she has made a preposition, they politely go to the house together and look the girl over without concealment, and in front of all the relationships.'

They understood, but they answered that they had no conversational women and followed no such custom, and Lefty said, 'That's all the better, because if you go in for that kind of thing you have to do it with a circumstantial intention, and since I don't feel none towards a foreign nation, what's the use of stringing the girls along?'

The Englishmen were pleased with him for these opinions too, and so they started off again in their friendly way, slapping him on the back and the knees, and they asked: 'Just out of curiosity,' they said, 'we'd like to know what signs of defects you've noticed in our girls, and why you keep away from them?'

At this Lefty answered them frankly, 'I don't mean to run them down; I just don't like the way their dresses sort of swish back and forth, so that you can't make out just what they've got on and what it's for. There'll be one thing here, and below something else will be pinned on, and on their arms they'll have some kind of socks. In them velveteen coats of theirs they look just like capuchin monkeys.'

The Englishmen laughed and said, 'Why does that get in your way?'

'It don't get in my way,' answered Lefty, 'only I'm scared I'd be ashamed to look and wait until she got untangled from all that stuff.'

'But do you really think your fashions are better?' they asked.

'Our fashions in Tula,' he replied, 'are simple: every girl is dressed in her own lace. Our lace is worn even by fine ladies.'

Then they showed him off to their own ladies, and there they served him tea and asked him, 'What are you frowning for?'

He answered that 'We ain't used to drinking it so sweet.'

Then they served it to him in the Russian way, with a lump of sugar to suck.

This didn't seem to be as good to them, but Lefty said, 'To our taste this way it's tastier.'

The Englishmen couldn't find any bait at all that could make him take to their life. They could only talk him into staying with them for a short while as their guest, and said they would take him to all sorts of factories and show him all their arts.

And after that, they said, they would put him on their own ship and 'deliver him safe and sound in Petersburg.'

He agreed to that.

### 16

The Englishmen took charge of Lefty and sent the Russian courier back to Russia. Even though the courier had government rank and was learned in various languages, they weren't interested in him, but they *were* interested in Lefty, and they set out to take Lefty around and show him everything. He looked at all their production: he really liked their metallic mills and their soapy-rope factories, and the way they managed things – especially the way they took care of their workers. Every one of their workmen was always well fed, none was dressed in rags, each one had on a capable everyday jacket and wore thick hard-nail boots with iron caps, so that he wouldn't stump his toes anywhere on anything. Along with his work he got teaching instead of beatings, and he worked with comprehension. In front of each one, hung up right in full view, was a stultification table, and within arm's reach was a racing slate. Whatever any craftsman did, he would look up at the tables, and then check it with comprehension, and then write one thing down on the slate, race another thing, and put it together accurately: whatever was written down in the figures really came out that way. And when a holiday came, they would all get together in couples, each one would take a walking stick in his hand, and they would go for a walk in a proper way, all proud and polite.

Lefty got a good look at all their life and all their work, but above all else he paid attention to something that surprised the Englishmen a lot. He wasn't interested so much in how they made new rifles as in how they took care of the old ones. He would walk around everything and praise it and say, 'We can do that too.'

But whenever he came to an old rifle, he would stick his finger in the barrel, rub it around inside, and sigh, 'That is way yonder better than ours.'

The Englishmen couldn't figure out what Lefty noticed. He asked them, 'Might I know whether or not our generals have ever looked at this?'

They answered, 'Those who have been here must have taken a look.'

'But when they were here,' he asked, 'did they have gloves on or not?'

'Yours are full-dress generals,' they said. 'Gloves come with them, so they must have had them on here.'

43

Lefty said nothing. But suddenly he began to feel an uneasy homesickness. He pined away and pined away and said to the Englishmen, 'I thank you kindly for your entertainment, and I like everything in your country, and I've seen everything I needed to see – and now I'd like to go home in a hurry.' —

They couldn't hold him back any longer. There was no way to let him go by land because he didn't know all languages, and it was a bad time to go by sea because it was the fall of the year and stormy, but he insisted, 'Let me go.'

'We've looked at the whether-meter,' they said. 'A storm is coming; you could drown; after all, this is not like your Gulf of Finland – this is the real Militerranean Sea.'

'It's all the same where a man dies,' he answered. 'It's all God's will alone, and I want to get back home in a hurry; because if I don't, I might get a kind of craziness in the head.'

They couldn't hold him back by force. They fed him till he creaked, they rewarded him with money, they gave him an alarmed gold watch as a souvenir, and for the cold weather at sea on the late fall voyage they gave him a woollen overcoat with a windy hurricane hat for his head. They dressed him warmly and took him down to the ship that was sailing for Russia. There they gave Lefty the very best cabin, like a real nobleman, but he felt ashamed and didn't like to sit shut up with the other gentlemen, and he would go up on deck and sit down under the tar poling and ask, 'Where is our Russia?'

The Englishman he asked would point or nod off in that direction, and then Lefty would turn his head that way and impatiently look for his native land.

When they sailed out of the bay into the Militerranean Sea, his longing for Russia became so strong that there was no way to calm him down. The rolling and pitching was awful, but Lefty still wouldn't go down to his cabin; he sat under the tar poling, pulled his hurricane hat down over his eyes and kept looking towards his homeland.

Often the Englishmen would come up and invite him to a warm spot down below, and he even began to lie his way out so that they would stop bothering him. 'No,' he would answer. 'I feel better out here; if I went inside with all this rolling and pitching the sea wretch would get me.'

And so the whole time he would never go below until he had to for special reasons, and because of this the thirst mate took a liking to him. This thirst mate, to the misfortune of our Lefty, knew how to talk Russian, and he couldn't get over marvelling that a Russian landlubber could hold out like that through all the rough weather.

'Good lad, Russ!' he said. 'Let's take a drink!'

Lefty took a drink.

And the thirst mate said, 'Another one!'

So Lefty took another one, and they drank themselves tight. The thirst mate asked him, 'What kind of secret is it you're taking to Russia from our country?'

Lefty answered, 'That's my business.'

'Well, if that's the way it is,' answered the thirst mate, 'then let me make an English bet with you.'

Lefty asked, 'What kind?'

'That we'll never drink alone and will always drink the same – one just as much as the other – and whoever drinks the other one down will win.'

Lefty thought, 'Dark skies, bellies rise; the boredom's strong and the way is long. We still can't see the homeland beyond the waves – it will be merrier after all to make the bet.'

'All right,' he said. 'It's a bet.'

'Only let it be honest.'

'As far as that goes,' he said, 'you ain't got no worry.'

They agreed and shook hands on it.


17


Their bet began in the Militerranean Sea, and they drank all the way to the Riga Dunamunde, but they ran neck and neck, and neither one fell behind the other, and they kept so strictly even with each other that when one of them looked down into the sea and saw a devil climbing up out of the water, the very same thing immediately appeared to the other one. Only, the thirst mate saw a red-headed devil, and Lefty claimed it was dark, like a blackamoor.

Lefty said, 'Cross yourself and turn away; that's a devil from the deep.'

But the Englishman argued that it was only a 'deep-sea driver'. 'If you want me to,' he said, 'I'll pitch you overboard. Don't be afraid – he'll bring you right back to me.'

And Lefty answered, 'If that's true, then pitch me over.'

The thirst mate picked him up by the shoulders and carried him to the rail.

The sailors saw this and stopped them and reported it to the captain. He ordered them both to be locked up below and kept on rations of rum and wine and cold food, so that they could both eat and drink and stick to their bet, but he gave orders that they were not to get any hot glum pudding in flames, for fear the spirits in their innards might catch fire.

So they travelled locked up all the way to Petersburg, and neither one of them won the bet. There they were spread out in separate sleighs, and the Englishman was sent to the embassy on the English quay and Lefty to the police station.

From this point their destinies became very different.

18

When the Englishman was brought to the Ambassador's house, they at once called in a doctor and a druggist for him. The doctor ordered him put into a warm bath on the spot, and the druggist right away rolled up a gutta-percha pill and personally stuck it in his mouth, and then both of them together took and laid him on a feather bed and covered him over with a fur coat and left him to sweat; and to keep anyone from disturbing him the order was sent out through the whole embassy to let nobody sneeze. The doctor and the druggist waited till the thirst mate went to sleep, and then they made another gutta-percha pill for him, laid it on a little table at the head of his bed and went off.

But at the police station they threw Lefty on the floor and started questioning him, 'Who was he, and where was he from, and did he have a grasp port or any other kind of document?'

But he was so weak from his illness and the drinking and the rolling and pitching that he didn't answer a word, but only groaned.

Then they searched him right away, relieved him of his colourful clothes and his alarmed watch and fleeced him of his money; and the police officer gave orders that the first passing sleigh-driver should take him free to the hospital.

The policeman took Lefty out to put him into a sleigh, but for a long time he couldn't catch a single one, because sleigh-drivers avoid policemen. Lefty was lying all this time on the cold depravement. Then the policeman caught a sleigh-driver, only one without a warm fur lap-robe, because in cases like that they hide the fur lap-robe by sitting on it, in order to make policemen's feet freeze faster. So they carried Lefty in an open sleigh, and whenever they transferred him from one sleigh to another they would keep dropping him, and when they picked him up they would pull his ears to make him come to. They got him to one hospital, but there they wouldn't accept him without a grasp port; they took him to another, and they wouldn't accept him there either; and then to a third, and a fourth. All night long they kept dragging him through all the little winding alleys and transferring him over and over, until he was half dead. Then one doctor's assistant told the policeman to take him to the Obukhvin Public Hospital, where everybody of unknown social class was taken in to die.

There they gave orders to write out a receipt and deposit Lefty on the floor in the corridor till they could inspect him.

And at that very same time the next day the English thirst mate got up, swallowed the second gutta-percha pill down to his innards, ate a light breakfast of chicken and rice, took a drink of impressed air, and said, 'Where is my Russian buddy? I'm going to look for him.'

19

He got dressed and off he ran.

In some amazing way the thirst mate found Lefty very quickly; only, they hadn't yet put him on a bed. He was still lying in the hall on the floor, and he complained to the Englishman. 'I've just got to have two words with the Emperor,' he said.

The Englishman ran off to Count Kleinmichel and ripped and roared, 'Really, now, this is the limit!' he said. 'Though only a sheep-skin coat it be, in its wearer a human soul we see.'

For this statement the Englishman was turned out at once, so that he shouldn't dare mention the human soul again. After that somebody said to him, 'You'd do better to go around to Platov the Cossack; he's got simple feelings.'

The Englishman got hold of Platov, who by this time was lying again on his bed. Platov listened to his story and remembered Lefty.

'Why, of course, brother,' he said. 'I know him very well. I've even dragged him around by the hair. Only, I don't know how I can help him in this kind of trouble, because I've served out my time and got a full apple plexy – now they don't pay attention to me any more. But you just run over to the Commandant Skobelev; he's in full force, and he's also had experience in this line – he'll do something.'

The thirst mate went to Skobelev and told all about what sort of illness Lefty had and how it had happened. Skobelev said, 'I understand that illness; only, the Germans don't know how to treat it; here you have to have some kind of doctor from the spiritual profession, because they have grown up with these cases and they can help; I'll send over the Russian doctor Martyn-Solsky right away.'

But when Martyn-Solsky got there, Lefty was already dying, because he had cracked open the back of his head when they dropped him on the cold depravement; and he was able to say only one thing clearly, 'Tell the Emperor that the English don't clean their rifles with brick dust, and we must stop it too, or else God save us from a war, because they won't be any good for shooting.'

And with this loyalty, Lefty crossed himself and kicked the bucket.

Martyn-Solsky went out at once and reported this to Count Chernyshov, so that he could tell the Emperor, but Count Chernyshov shouted at him, 'Look here now,' he said, 'your job is laxatives and purgatives. Don't stick your nose into other people's business: in Russia we've got generals for that.'

So nothing was said to the Emperor, and the cleaning went on in the same old way right up to the Crimean War. At that time when they started loading their rifles, the bullets just rattled around in them, because the barrels had been cleaned out with brick dust.

Then Martyn-Solsky reminded Count Chernyshov about Lefty, and Count Chernyshov said, 'Go to the devil, you public enema, and don't stick your nose into other people's business or I'll deny I ever heard about that from you, and then you yourself will catch it.'

Martyn-Solsky thought, 'And he really will deny it.' So he kept quiet.

But if only they had reported Lefty's words in time to the Emperor, the war against the enemy in Crimea would have taken an entirely different turn.

Now all this is 'affairs of long-gone days' and 'traditions of yore' even though this yore is not very old. But there is no need to be hasty about forgetting these traditions, despite the incredible nature of the legend and the epic character of its principal hero. Lefty's real name, like the names of many of the greatest geniuses, has been lost to posterity forever; but he is interesting as the embodiment of a myth in the popular imagination, and his adventures can serve to remind us of an epoch whose general spirit has been portrayed here clearly and accurately.

It goes without saying that Tula no longer has such master craftsmen as the legendary Lefty: machines have evened up the inequalities in gifts and talents, and genius no longer strains itself in a struggle against diligence and exactness. Even though they encourage the raising of salaries, machines do not encourage artistic daring, which sometimes went so far beyond ordinary bounds as to inspire the folk imagination to create unbelievable legends like this one.

The workmen, of course, can appreciate the advantages they have gained through practical applications of mechanical science, but they still recall those olden times with pride and affection. These memories are their epic – an epic that has a genuinely 'human soul'.